The Beautiful Lady
Our Lady
of Guadalupe

by

Pat Mora

illustrated by

Steve Johnson & Lou Fancher

Alfred A. Knopf ⚬ New York

THIS IS A BORZOI BOOK PUBLISHED BY ALFRED A. KNOPF

Text copyright © 2012 by Pat Mora

Jacket art and interior illustrations copyright © 2012 by Steve Johnson and Lou Fancher

All rights reserved. Published in the United States by Alfred A. Knopf,
an imprint of Random House Children's Books, a division of Random House, Inc., New York.
Knopf, Borzoi Books, and the colophon are registered trademarks of Random House, Inc.
Visit us on the Web! randomhouse.com/kids
Educators and librarians, for a variety of teaching tools, visit us at RHTeachersLibrarians.com

Library of Congress Cataloging-in-Publication Data
Mora, Pat.
The beautiful lady : Our Lady of Guadalupe / by Pat Mora ; illustrated by Steve Johnson and Lou Fancher. — 1st ed.
p. cm.
Summary: Grandma Lupita tells her granddaughter Rose and Rose's friend Terry the story of Our Lady of Guadalupe,
a miracle that occurred near Mexico City in 1531. Includes facts about the event and its influence.
ISBN 978-0-375-86838-2 (trade) — ISBN 978-0-375-96838-9 (lib. bdg.)
1. Guadalupe, Our Lady of—Juvenile fiction. [1. Guadalupe, Our Lady of—Fiction. 2. Aztecs—Fiction. 3. Indians of Mexico—Fiction.
4. Miracles—Fiction. 5. Mexico—History—16th century—Fiction.] I. Johnson, Steve, ill.
II. Fancher, Lou, ill. III. Title.
PZ7.M78819Be 2013
[E]—dc23
2011040784

MANUFACTURED IN CHINA
December 2012   10 9 8 7 6 5 4 3 2 1   First Edition

In memory of my father, Raúl Antonio Mora,
who loved Our Lady of Guadalupe; and of my friend,
Rose Treviño, a fine librarian and literacy advocate
—P.M.

For Nick
—S.J. and L.F.

"Look! I did it!" Terry holds up a bright red paper flower.

"*Gracias*, Grandma Lupita, for teaching Terry to make these," I say.

"I used to make flowers like this with my grandmother in Mexico," says Grandma Lupita. "When we'd go to the market holding hands, we'd see huge paper flowers— yellow, orange, and red, like those in the living room. I'm so happy you girls came on this cold December day, *mis queridas*."

"Who's that pretty lady?" asks Terry. "I like all the gold stars on her cloak. I like her face, too."

"That's Our Lady of Guadalupe, and today is her special day," says Grandma. "Every December, Rose and I make pretty flowers to put around the statue."

And every December, Grandma Lupita tells me the story of Our Lady of Guadalupe.

"Long ago," Grandma begins, "on a cold December morning near what is now Mexico City, a man named Juan Diego put on his *tilma*, his cloak, and started down the road to church. As he walked along, he heard lovely bird songs swirling through the air at the top of Tepeyac Hill.

"Curious, Juan Diego looked up. Suddenly all the birds were silent. Juan Diego heard only the wind. Then, at the top of the hill, Juan Diego saw a shining bright light."

Grandma carefully pulls the folded paper she's holding into red petals.

"Please, don't stop," says Terry. "What happened?"

Grandma smiles. "Like morning sunlight, as if the sun had slid down to the earth, the hill glowed.

"In the middle of all that soft light was a beautiful lady," says Grandma, picking up the statue. "Her cloak shone with stars. She was floating on a sliver of moon. Her skin was brown and beautiful. The Lady smiled.

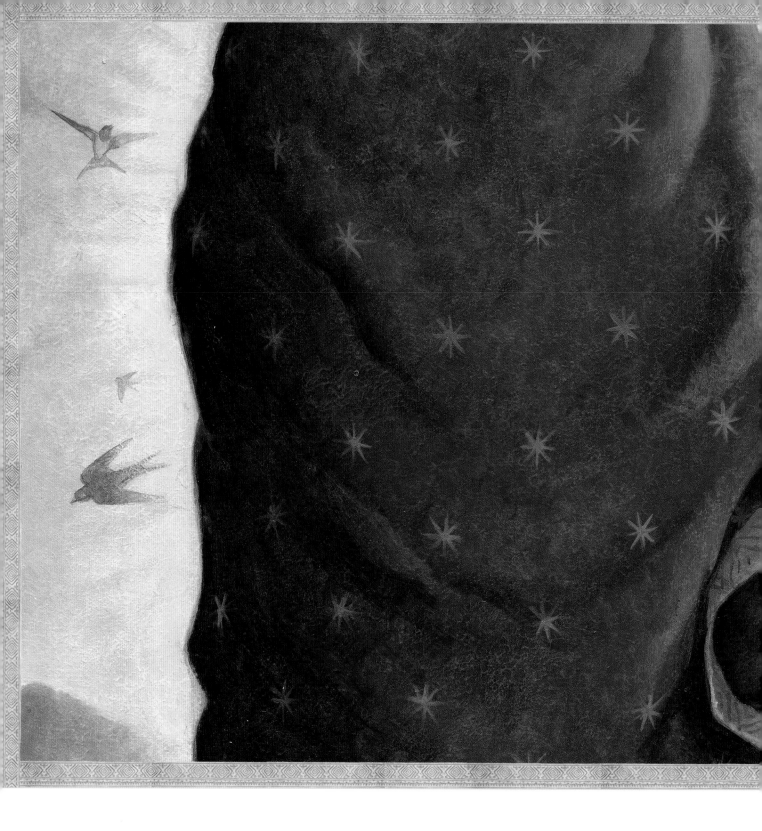

"Juan Diego wondered, who was this lady surrounded by light?
"'Juan Diego,' said the Lady. Her voice was like a song, like
river music.

"The Lady asked Juan Diego to go visit the bishop in the nearby
city and ask him to build a special church for her on the hilltop. She
wanted a place where people could rest and pray.

"Juan Diego started down the dirt path. He was a good man and wanted to do as the Lady asked, but he didn't know the bishop, who was a very important man. When Juan Diego arrived at the palace, many people were waiting to speak to the bishop. Juan Diego stood quietly. He waited, and waited, and waited.

"'I don't want to disappoint the beautiful *Señora*,' thought Juan Diego. Finally, it was his turn to say a few words to the bishop. The bishop listened. He thought. But then he said he needed a sign, proof from *la hermosa Señora*.

"Juan Diego wished he could build the church himself. He walked home slowly. He went softly by Tepeyac Hill, hoping he wouldn't see the Lady again. He didn't want to tell her that the bishop was not ready to build her a church.

"'Juanito,' called the Lady. Juan Diego looked up and saw the beautiful Lady. Rays of light shone behind her.

"Then Juan Diego looked down sadly. 'Ay, *Señora*, I feel embarrassed,' he said. 'The bishop asked for a sign from you. Maybe you should ask a rich and important person to talk to the bishop. I am a poor man and have no influence.'

"The kind Lady smiled. 'Juanito,' she said, 'you are a good man. I want you to go speak to the bishop again and ask him to build my church. Here. On this hill.'

"The next morning, Juan Diego again put on his *tilma* and went to see the bishop. He waited, and waited, and waited. He wanted to make the kind and beautiful *Señora* happy. Finally, it was his turn.

"The bishop listened and said, '*Por favor*, bring me a sign from the Lady.'

"Juan Diego left the bishop's palace. He walked softly by
Tepeyac Hill, but again he heard a voice sweet as river music.
'Juanito, *por favor*. Return to the bishop tomorrow.'

"That night, Juan Diego sat on his favorite rock and looked up at his favorite stars and at the sliver of moon. He looked at the sky, his comfort night after night. He looked at the silhouettes of the volcanoes and hills. He thought of the sparrows, lizards, corn, and rocks sleeping around him in the dark. They reminded him of his mother, who had loved *las estrellas* and *la luna,* too.

"He thought about *la Señora*. She was kind and gentle, like his mother. With light around her, stars on her cloak, and a sliver of the moon under her feet, *la Señora* was beautiful, like the earth and all the light around it. Juan Diego said his prayers. He wanted to wake up and help build the church for *la Señora*, but the bishop needed a sign from her.

"The next day, Juan Diego watched the sun rise and thought about the light around the beautiful Lady. He put on his *tilma* and set off on a different path, hoping the Lady wouldn't see him. He watched snow lightly begin to fall.

"'Juanito,' he heard again. Juan Diego saw the Lady coming down the hill toward him.

"'I am so sorry, *Señora*,' said Juan Diego softly, 'but the bishop needs a sign from you.'

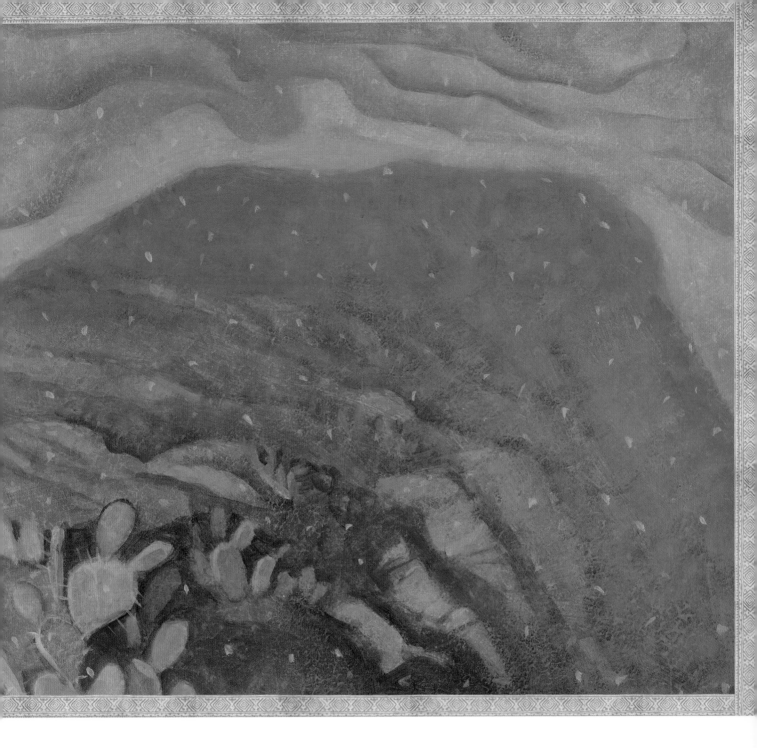

"Like a kind mother, the Lady smiled and pointed. 'Go,' she said.
'In your *tilma*, bring me flowers growing at the top of the hill.'

"'The cactus?' asked Juan Diego.

"The Lady smiled again. 'The flowers, Juanito,' she said.

"Juan Diego thought, 'It is winter. How can there be flowers?'
But Juan Diego climbed.

"'Oh, *Señora!*' he gasped. The plants glowed like jewels. The hilltop gleamed with tiny rainbows! And Juan Diego saw roses, *rosas hermosas*, blooming red in the snow. Slowly, he gathered flowers in his *tilma* and took them down to the Lady.

"Carefully, she arranged the roses in Juan Diego's cloak.
'There,' she said. 'Take those to the bishop.'

"Juan Diego ran cautiously so as not to drop the flowers. When he rushed into the bishop's palace, everyone stopped. Everyone looked at him. In all that sudden silence, Juan Diego opened his cloak. He couldn't wait for the bishop and everyone to see the roses from the beautiful lady.

"As the roses tumbled out, their sweet scent floated around the room. Then everyone pointed at Juan Diego's *tilma*. He looked down. There, on his cloak, was the image of *la hermosa Señora*! Everyone saw her and the sun's rays, the stars on her green cloak, and how she floated on a sliver of moon.

"Then," says Grandma, "Juan Diego carefully touched her beautiful brown face."

"The end!" I say.

Grandma smiles and pats my hand. She touches the face of Our Lady of Guadalupe. Grandma says, "Many people now visit Our Lady's famous church. They look up and see Juan Diego's *tilma*, and they see the gentle face of Our Lady of Guadalupe."

Grandma, Terry, and I put our flowers around the statue.

"I love that story, Grandma!" I say. "Your name is Lupita, so this is your special day, too, right?"

Grandma hugs me and says, "Rose, Terry, I have a surprise for you." She takes us to the kitchen.

"Look!" says Terry. "Rose cookies!"

"They smell delicious, Grandma!" I say. "Roses in December, a party to celebrate Our Lady of Guadalupe."

Author's Note: Our Lady of Guadalupe

One of Mexico's most loved stories is the miracle of Our Lady of Guadalupe. In December 1531, on the hill of Tepeyac in what is now Mexico City, Nuestra Señora de Guadalupe, the best-known manifestation of Mary in the Americas, appeared to an Aztec villager named Juan Diego. She requested that he go to the bishop and ask him to build a church for her. The story says that the bishop initially didn't believe Juan Diego and asked for a sign.

Historically and to the present, the image of Our Lady of Guadalupe is a powerful symbol for Mexicans, people of Mexican descent, Latinos, Catholics, and all who find comfort in her. Her image was carried in Mexico's War of Independence (1810) and is still carried today as a symbol of freedom and justice by groups struggling for their rights, such as farmworkers in the United States. Her original basilica, completed in 1709, replaced previous churches at the site as devotion to Our Lady grew. Next to it is the modern basilica (opened in 1976) of Nuestra Señora de Guadalupe, one of the most popular pilgrimage sites in the Americas.

People around the world, from diverse backgrounds and economic levels, come to seek her help, to fulfill a promise, and to gaze at Juan Diego's cloak, or *tilma*, which miraculously still has Our Lady's image preserved on the cactus-fiber cloth. On December 12, her feast day, millions visit the site. In 2002, the Catholic Church canonized Juan Diego as the first indigenous saint of the Americas.

Our Lady of Guadalupe is also known as la Virgen Morena (the Brown-Skinned Virgin), la Reina de las Américas (the Queen of the Americas), and the Protectress of New Mexico. Our Lady is celebrated in public art, churches, museums, and homes, not only on canvases, murals, and sculptures, but also in pop-culture items including calendars, car decals, souvenirs, tattoos, mouse pads, T-shirts, and coloring books.

On a personal note, a large image of Our Lady of Guadalupe always hung in my parents' bedroom. She is the patient and loving mother who watches over her dark-skinned children, as well as all who call on her.